DEATH OF THE
HEART
BROKEN

DEATH OF THE HEART BROKEN

CHUONG VAN NGUYEN

Death Of The Heart Broken

Copyright © 2023 by Chuong van Nguyen. All rights reserved.

No part of this publication may be reproduced, stored in a retrieval system or transmitted in any way by any means, electronic, mechanical, photocopy, recording or otherwise without the prior permission of the author except as provided by USA copyright law.

The opinions expressed by the author are not necessarily those of URLink Print and Media.

1603 Capitol Ave., Suite 310 Cheyenne, Wyoming USA 82001
1-888-980-6523 | admin@urlinkpublishing.com

URLink Print and Media is committed to excellence in the publishing industry.

Book design copyright © 2023 by URLink Print and Media. All rights reserved.

Published in the United States of America

ISBN 978-1-68486-501-7 (Paperback)
ISBN 978-1-68486-431-7 (Digital)

22.04.23

DEATH OF THE HEART BROKEN

Once upon a time, there was a beautiful young age seventeen-year-old girl name "Kasumi" from Japan.

She also has a younger sister the age of sixteen name "Mai."

The two sisters were studying in school in the time being but had to quit and leave early due to their mother being sick all the sudden. She is now in the hospital for treatment and couldn't take care of the pair so they're going to their fathers temporary home for now until she gotten better, and they will return back to her once she is fully recovered.

When Kasumi and Mai are on their way to their fathers, they bought the famous Sakuma fruit drops candy to eat. Due to travelling a far range distance, they had finally found and made it to their fathers place, and didn't expected to think what it was going to be. They didn't know at first that it was going to be living in a farm that is so isolated and far from everything, but they knew it was just only going to be temporary living there.

The two daughters just stand there and look at him strangely because they had never really met him since they were little babies.

He told the girls that they must be his two daughters "Kasumi and Mai."

They replied Yes! At ease.

The father then showed them around the house first including their rooms, then later the farm. Once he is finished with that, he later showed his backyard filled full of crops and poultry.

The father asks the girls if they like what they have seen so far. They think it's nice and beautiful here. He further explains to them that this is only temporary and they would be back to their mothers in no time after she is well again.

"They know already, said the two girls!"

In the meantime, the two Kasumi and Mai was wandering the place checking the farm out. They were kind of excited to see the land animals and crops. Kasumi then comes to the fruit isle and hand picking the fruit that she chose. She picked the strawberries from the plant tree and tasted them. She loved it very much the sweetness and the taste. She also tells Mai to pick and eat them as well. So, she did.

"Delicious, said she!" in a mouthwatering way!

After the two having fun picking and eating fruits, they head back inside the house going into their own rooms. They both were trying to finish unpacking their luggage's. while they were unpacking, from Kasumi's side, she took out the portrait of her favorite idol which was a Hongkong movie star from China descent and held his picture into her arms. He's name is Ian Cheung and she loves him with all her heart. She will even die for him that she claims.

Since she is Japanese, she doesn't mind that he's Chinese at all. She knows the Chinese and the Japanese don't associate with each other due to the past war but knows it is long time ago and a lot of them have moved on.

She is just sitting there looking at the picture of him for long time until her sister came standing at her door room unexpectedly.

"Who is that guy your keep on staring at in the portrait Mai asks!"

"It's Ian Cheung a famous Hongkong actor she replies!"

"Gross, said she." A Chinese man!

Kasumi then shows the picture of him with a closer look.

"Oh, wow he does look pretty, Mai says."

Anyhow Kasumi wonders and said to her if a guy like Ian Cheung would be into Japanese girls.

"Don't know, Mai said."

She explains to her further that she wants to meet him one day if he ever comes to Japan for tour visits. It would be a big special day for her if he does.

Their father then comes in the room and breaks up the conversation, asking them to go out and have some lunch that he made. And so, they went!

While munching on the food, the father asks the girls if they would like to go shopping with him later on after they had finish eating.

The girls have agreed and decided to go. He warns them that by going there, it is a long hours' drive by using he's truck!

They understand and still went anyways. So now they're heading off. A few hours later, they had arrived to the shops. The father knows the daughters don't have much cash on them due to their trip to his home from their mothers. He gave some money to them to go around and buy some certain things that could come in handy. The two girls then walks around looking at the shops but don't know what they could spend with such a petty cash that their father gave. Until they see and went into the bicycle store. They know they don't have the money to buy a bike, but they might as well went in anyway just to take a look around. They suddenly see a bicycle that they like both. Kasumi likes the light green colored bike and Mai likes the light pink one. They so badly wish they could buy them but knowing that they can't afford it. The price of the bicycle's is just too high for them to even purchase. The girls were then about to leave the store until they over heard the other customers talking about Ian Cheung her idol is coming to Japan in this town.

Kasumi comes to them and jumps into their conversation asking is Ian Cheung the Hongkong superstar coming here to Japan in this town!

They replied with a yes!

"Wow its like a dream come true Kasumi says, in a very happy exciting way!"

She continues to ask them if they know when the exact date that he would be arriving?

They don't have any idea when exactly he would be coming but they know it would be soon that they heard the rumor.

And that was it for the conversation. Kasumi and Mai walked out of the store feeling full of happiness to know that Ian Cheung would be coming to this town.

They both were walking along back to look for their father, until some blokes came up to them sexual harassing the two. One of the guy name Ren tried to asks Kasumi out but she refuses, so he tried to ask her out by using force on her. He grabbed her arm demanding her to come with him on a date. She tried to fight back but couldn't do much when her father came into the rescue and stopped it. He twisted Ren's arm from behind and pushes him away. He then took out he's shotgun from the truck and tried scaring them so they could leave!

Ren and the boys told him and he's daughters that this isn't over and fled the scene. The father asks the girls are they alright and they replied with a yes!

They all went home together afterwards.

When they were going home, the Ren guy and he's boys were following him from behind on their cars without them even noticing it.

When the father and the daughters have arrived back home with hours drive, the boys from behind them now knows exactly where they live at. They leave it for now and head back home. Ren said he will get them back at some point.

Hours from the shops, the three all the sudden have gotten very hungry again, so they made sashimi for their dinner. They'd enjoy their food that evening.

While eating the father was discussing to the girls. He wanted to know if the girls would want a part time job working for him in this farm of his.

They didn't know at first the reason why they should work but the father explains to them that they should do it for the money to go and buy things and that it is only for temporary until their mother is feeling better, then they get to quit and move back home to her.

The daughters look at each other determining whether if they would want to work as a part timer or not. They both then agreed because they know themselves that's its only going to be whiles work but not forever.

Later that night, the daughters took a good rest preparing for tomorrow's work.

The following morning, the girls woke up preparing for their early start. Waiting for the father to help mentor them.

He is up and ready to start work.

Besides he the girls thought it would be him that would be teaching them how to process the animals and harvest crops. It turns out the father wanted the employees of the farm to teach them along the way not him.

So during the day, the workers help mentoring the girls out a bit and then worked independently afterwards.

During their end of the four-hour shift, the father asks them how did it go? The girls reply with a happy yes, they loved it and thinks that it is very fun job to do but a bit exhausting at first because they're beginners on the day.

"Everybody is helpful and polite said Mai!"

The girls then asks him how many hours in a shift does he and the other employees work for? Ten hours he replies!

"Wow that is a long hour shift, Kasumi says!"

He then told the girls to go take a rest for the day and prepare for the next following day and the day after until its end of the Friday.

Days of working, they have came down to the end of the week. The father told the girls to come and collect their payday.

He has calculated the two girl's hours earning. It was a total of twenty hours each in their first start of the week.

Kasumi and Mai took the money and counted it with excitement as they have never held this amount of money before ever in their life for their age. They were so happy to have made an amount of money that can afford to go buy the bicycles that they saw last week. By working and getting so much money from the farm the girls are started to feel addicted.

They ask the father if he could take them to go and buy their favorite bicycle at the shop.

He insisted and left the farm for the other workers to take in charge of while he is gone to take the girls out to the shops that afternoon.

When the father had driven them long hours to the bicycle shop, he finally has arrived there.

The girls quickly rushed into the store and got the ones they saw a week ago. The light green bicycle which is Kasumi's and the other light pink one is for Mai's. they got the bikes and went to the salesman and paid the Man.

The father loaded the two bicycles on the truck and driven it back home with his daughters.

When they had gotten back home Kasumi and Mai were so anxious to ride the bikes. They ask the father permission for them to take the bikes and ride them on the road.

He said yes and told them to be careful!

They then ride along the roads watching out carefully for any up coming vehicles. They were enjoying riding around with their happy smiles on their faces, they loved it very much to just how new and smooth it goes.

While riding around for a time being, they headed back home feeling hungry. The father told the girls to put the bicycles away and come in the house to get ready for dinner time.

When they were inside having dinner, he asks the girls about the question if they still wanting to continue working because they already have gotten what they wanted.

They struggle at first don't know what to answer, because they don't know what else they could spend the money on if they keep working for more.

He gave advice to them explaining that they should never quit continuing working because they never know they might need the money for something else in a matter of hand.

They thought about it for a moment and agreed what he says. They continue to work for him on a following Monday. After their conversation, they all went to bed.

The next day, during the weekend the two Kasumi and Mai taken their bicycles out for a ride again away from the farm, while in the meantime the father went to go get some more food for the animals from a distance to his house.

When they all left the farm, Ren and he's boys were hiding in a spot where they could not be seen by them. they then went in and stormed the farm wrecking and destroying everything in their path.

The workers that are working overtime were shocked to see that a bunch of disguised boys raiding the entire farm. The workers tried to talk them out of it but failed to do so. There wasn't much they could do due to their weapons they were carrying.

While the boys were doing their part, Ren went inside of the house looking for Kasumi's room so he could mess it up further until he sees a portrait on the cupboard. He looks at it and recognized the guy in the photo.

"The famous Hongkong star, he has said!"

He knows the picture of Ian Cheung and he too also knows that he is coming into town.

In he's mind he suddenly came up with an evil plan. He then threw the portrait on the ground and stepped on it until it breaks the glass. He walks out of the house and called all the boys back. He told them to all leave with him.

When they had left the premise, the workers were shocked and called the police. They also rang the boss to let him know what on earth is happening to his farm. He now got informed and is heading back asap.

While the father is heading back, Kasumi and Mai are too busy having fun enjoying themselves not knowing about the situation. They later head back home with an unexpected look on their faces. They weren't so surprised to be seeing cops everywhere surrounding at their home. They can see one of them are speaking to their father. The daughters came up to him asking him what is going on?

He explains to the girls that the farm was under attack by some young blokes dressed in black a while ago!

And the way how it's been described, the father feels suspicious of the suspects but cannot bring them into justice. He hasn't got the proof yet to show evidence to the cops.

He kept to himself the father knowing that it feels like the boys that were sexual harassing he's daughters at the shops, must of followed through all the way to here without even noticing it.

The girls then went out the back and seen so many damage crops and a few dead animals. They were deeply sad to see what has happen to this place.

This whole incident is now been reported and the police have left the scene.

The father later tells everybody to go back to work like what they usually do and he will go clean up the mess. He also tells the girls to go clean up inside of the house for him especially their rooms.

Once they have done all that already, Mai enters into Kasumi's room after they finishing tidying up. They were talking about the problem and turning on the television at the same time. While they were talking, they could hear on the television about her Idol Ian Cheung. The presenter on live tv can be heard saying that he will be coming to town this following week on a upcoming Saturday.

The two are exciting to hear the news. They never thought that the rumor would be true. He is really coming to Japan after all.

Kasumi turned off the television and was happy. They went outside to further help their father cleaning out the farm that were damage.

Hours of cleaning, everything went back to the way things were again. Everybody went back to doing their duties while the two girls are off on the weekends.

Then seven days later, the girls got super excited to be seeing her Idol to be coming to town. Kasumi was so excited that she even forgot to collect her payday of the week. Her sister had to handed to her the money.

Kasumi asks the father if he could drive them to town to see Ian Cheung.

"Absolutely, he said!"

They were even more happy and thanked him.

They are now all packed up and ready to go. They hopped on the truck and started the ignition when suddenly it did not work and end up stalling.

"this cannot be happening right now, Kasumi says" in a panic way!

The father apologized to the girls knowing there is no other else he can do to take them to town to see Ian Cheung.

Kasumi then asks him for permission if she could take her bicycle and ride there herself.

He lets her but telling she that it will take probably triple the trip to get there to town.

"It's going to take hours, he says." Still up for it!

She rushes him in a way and quickly hops on the bicycle. She then also asks Mai if she is also coming too but she said she pass because knowing just how far its going to get to it.

Kasumi loves Ian Cheung very badly and do what it takes to see him, so Mai is out of the question.

Kasumi has got no time to lose, and ride as fast as she possibly could. The two wished her the best of luck on getting there on time.

When Kasumi is trying to make her way there, on the other hand, Ren and the boys are already there in town. they can see Ian

Cheung in town walking and greeting to a lot of fans along the streets.

While they were watching him, Ren explains to the boys that the chick Kasumi loves him. He knows this because of the picture he saw in the portrait from her room that they raided in.

"Funny thing, Ren said!" if she truly loves this superstar then why isn't she here?

The other boys said that she might be running late probably.

"Anyways if she shows up then we will kill Ian Cheung in front of her, said Ren!"

About a few hours later, still no sign of her coming?

Ian Cheung has already left the town and on to his next one, which is quite far away from this one.

Ren and he's boys were feeling quite odd to not see Kasumi coming here to see her favorite Idol. All the fans have left, and everybody was shopping like they usually do. They were about to leave the boys until they suddenly see Kasumi!

She was very late!

Ren told the crew to hide themselves from her so she wouldn't spot them with suspicious!

When they were all hiding from her, they can see she look to be disappointed. Disappointed that she is too late and that her Idol is long gone.

She went around asking the people along the streets when did he leave town and they told her about just almost half an hour ago to the next town.

She understood and knows herself that he is long gone and she could not make it in time chasing after him.

She suddenly gave up and headed back home feeling like it's the end of the world.

She so badly wanted to meet up with him personally to see if Ian Cheung would like a

Japanese girl like her or not. She thinks to herself that she is very pretty but doesn't know if he thinks the same to her if he does see her.

When she goes back home, Ren and the boys now went to the next town to see Kasumi's Idol, following him to kill her lover.

Hours later, the father and Mai is waiting for Kasumi to head back home to hear the good news but unfortunately it was a bad one. She came back with the sad news.

She didn't have to explain it to them and they already know about the situation. They already know it was already too late to get to her Idol.

The father tried in a best way to cheer her up by asking her to have dinner, but she wasn't up for it and went in her room.

So, they went ahead and ate without Kasumi.

While eating and watching television, the news came up about Kasumi's Idol Ian Cheung!

He has been shot at multiple times by some young men. The tv reporter now shows the scene again that was captured live on camera as to what has happen earlier of how he got shot.

Kasumi can hear the news from out the dinner table and ran out to look at it. The three was in shocked to see and hear the news.

They also captured the guy that shot Ian Cheung, and he was a guy known as Ren!

"Isn't that the same bloke that was sexual harassing you girls at the store a while back ago, said the father!"

"yes, it was, said them!"

They continue to hear the news. The news reporter explaining, Ian Cheung is now in unstable condition and is being sent to the hospital for further treatment.

Kasumi couldn't bare to hear the bad news about her Idol, so she went back home feeling sad and depressed.

The next morning, they have received another unexpected news. It was about the mother from the hospital. The hospital called the father, and he went and told the news to the girls that their mother has passed away!

They were even more sad and depressed. They were suddenly crying now to know that she is gone for good. Which means they also know they won't be returning to their mother's home ever again.

Everybody was quiet for a moment sitting at the couch. The father turns on the tv trying to calm down the two girls, but none of them were paying attention to it until for a while the news about Ian Cheung pop up. The news reporter stated that he has now passed away and is no longer with us.

Kasumi couldn't bare to hear the news anymore. Two of her favorite human beings is now gone out of her life. She got very upset and scream very loudly smashing things on the way to getting her bicycle and riding out of the house.

She took the bike and ride far away as possible from her father's farm.

"where you going, said the father and Mai!"

She didn't respond back.

She is riding away while crying at the same time. She doesn't know where she is going but as far as she could, until she got to this place where there is a pond.

She put her bike down and went to the surface of the water and stood there in silence. She felt darkness and emptiness. Things were going so well lately, then the news about the death of her mom and her favorite Idol died, things went down the toilet.

Tears can be seen running down her eyes. Her final moment was in silence staring down at the pond.

Mai and the father gotten very worried to see that she hasn't returned back from home. It has gotten pretty dark and no sign of her. They know something doesn't feel right about her. They all thought she is just going somewhere to calm herself down. But since it's getting dark, they're getting kind of worried.

So, the two went out and search for her.

They were looking for her, but it was very hard to see because it was getting very dark. Moments of searching they finally can see her bicycle on the side of the road. They know she's close by somewhere.

They found her in lying in the pond.

It was already too late. She drowns herself to death.

The father pulled her out of the water and taken her back home crying with her other daughter Mai.

That night and until tomorrow, neither the father and Mai had any sleep. Mai was in Kasumi's room with her the whole time. And the father was sitting at the table. There was only one thing that he kept on thinking and which was stuck inside he's mind the entire time was killing Ren.

He didn't blame on his ex-wife for the death of Kasumi but blame it on Ren.

He then came into the room of Kasumi's and didn't expect what he was going to see. Another death of he's daughter Mai. She hangs herself from the fan top ceiling.

He took her down, hugging her crying with pain.

The only thing he could think of while holding onto he's daughter was killing Ren.

He then took a shotgun out of his closet and gotten out of the house and head to the police station to look for him. He was so frustrated that he could no longer think straight anymore.

Long hours of driving to search for Ren, he finally found him at the station.

He aimed and pointed the shot gun at Ren. The police officers told the father not to shoot but he did not listen, so the cops had no choice but to shoot him down.

He was on the ground but did not die from the bullets. He was badly injured and was taken away.

A few months later, he got recovered and discharged from the hospital by the doctors.

He finally went back home to his farm.

When he came home, he felt empty inside of him seeing that nobody is around. The only thing he could see is the animals and he's employees.

His daughters were all buried while he was in the hospital recovering. His employees taken good care of it. The funeral expenses were all paid for by them.

He came to the workers thanking them for everything while he was in the hospital. They said it is alright, don't mention it.

They also told him did he also hear about the news Ren guy that had got he's daughter all killed. He replied to them, no not yet.

He asks what happen to him and they told him he too also died as well. They said he got killed in prison by the other inmates. They said they heard it on the news saying that it was a conspiracy attack. They say it might be from the relatives of Ian Cheung.

He was so happy to hear the news about the death of Ren. He has finally got he's avenged by others.

The father of the daughters then suddenly gave a very big news to the employees. Telling them thanks for everything and that he will no longer be the boss of the farm and is giving it to them. he told them he could no longer work because of depression due to the death of his daughters.

Due to all the hard work that the employees did for him he now gave the entire farm to them. They understand his circumstance and accept his offer.

Later that day, he gave all the paperwork and contracts for them to sign.

Some time ago, he had moved out of the farm far away and lived in a unknown place. He too also died later due to depression. He committed suicide like he's daughters.

The end

www.ingramcontent.com/pod-product-compliance
Lightning Source LLC
LaVergne TN
LVHW021744060526
838200LV00052B/3464